The
Healing
Touch

JANET DAILEY

SIGNAL HILL

This book is fiction. The author invented the names, people, places, and events. If any of them are like real places, events, or people (living or dead), it is by chance.

SIGNAL HILL®

Copyright © 1994 by Janet Dailey
Signal Hill Publications
A publishing imprint of Laubach Literacy International
1320 Jamesville Avenue
Syracuse, NY 13210-0131

All rights reserved

Printed in the United States of America

Illustration by Cheri Bladholm
Original cover art by Ron Hall

9 8 7 6 5 4 3 2 1

Library of Congress Cataloging-in-Publication Data

Dailey, Janet.

The healing touch / Janet Dailey.

p. cm. — (Janet Dailey's love scenes)

ISBN 1-56420-099-X
I. Title. II. Series: Dailey, Janet. Janet Dailey's love scenes.

PS3554.A29H38   1994
813'.54—dc20

94-18397
CIP

The
Healing
Touch

Chapter 1

"I'm sorry to bother you at this time of night, Dr. Barclay," said the voice on the phone. "But we have an emergency here at Casa Colina."

Rebecca Barclay groaned as the words sank into her half-asleep brain. She rolled over in her bed and looked at the clock on her nightstand. Three o'clock in the morning.

"What seems to be the problem, Mr. O'Brien?" she asked, hoping it would be something simple.

"I have a nanny goat here who's having her first kid," the man replied. "Something's wrong. She's been at it for hours, and she's no further along."

A birthing. A *goat* birthing. Rebecca groaned again. It was never something simple at three o'clock in the morning.

She forced her voice to sound cheerful. "I'll be right there, Mr. O'Brien."

There's no rest for the weary, Rebecca thought as she hung up the phone. She crawled out of bed. She had only been asleep for an hour. She had spent her evening stitching up a big tomcat's chewed ears. He had lost a fight with an even bigger male, and he was in a very bad mood. Her left hand still stung from his scratches.

Rebecca was the only veterinarian in the small town of San Carlos who would make late-night house calls. As a result, she got hauled out of bed several times a week.

Exactly why did I want to be a vet? she asked herself as she pulled on jeans and a flannel shirt. *Wasn't it something about helping sick animals, relieving suffering, healing the wounded?*

Ugh! Right now, she didn't want to see another furry face for at least a month.

Grabbing her case full of drugs and instruments, she hurried out to her battered old pickup. For a brief moment she breathed in the sweet smell of the California summer night. The scent of the star jasmine planted beside her door blended with the orange blossoms from a grove nearby.

The night was silent and cool. Not a single headlight shone on the highway in front of the house. The town was asleep except for her and Mr. O'Brien— and, of course, that poor little nanny who was struggling to deliver her first baby.

"I'll be right there, sweetie," Rebecca whispered as she pulled out of her driveway. "Just hang on. Help is on the way."

Chapter 2

Ten minutes later, Rebecca arrived at Casa Colina, a lavish estate on the edge of San Carlos. The huge house gleamed blue-white in the moonlight. The old-fashioned Spanish hacienda had a red tiled roof and graceful arches covered with climbing roses.

Rebecca parked the truck in front of the house and got out. She knew the place well. As a child, she had played here many times. The Flores family had five daughters, and she had been friends with all of them.

Over the years, the girls had grown up and left home. Two winters ago, José and Rosa Flores had sold Casa Colina and moved to a smaller house in town.

Rebecca had been told that the new owners were private people. But she had heard little else about them. She was glad that they had kept Johnny O'Brien as their caretaker. He had worked at the casa for the past twenty years, and Rebecca liked him. He had a big Irish smile and a corny joke for everyone. She always enjoyed his company.

With her bag in hand, she hurried around the house toward the stables. A light burned in one window, throwing a golden glow across the lawns. She rushed inside and hoped she wasn't too late.

Johnny was kneeling beside a small white nanny goat who was lying on a pile of straw. The animal was breathing hard and straining. There was no sign of a new arrival.

Rebecca was so intent on her patient that she didn't notice the little girl who sat huddled in the corner of the stall. She was hugging her knees, which were drawn up to her chest. Her big blue eyes were filled with tears.

"How long has she been at it?" Rebecca asked. She knelt down next to the goat and ran her hand over its belly.

"Since this morning," Johnny replied, wiping his brow with a red kerchief. "Nothing's happened. Something must be tangled up in there."

"I believe you're right." Rebecca opened her bag and took out a tube of antiseptic cream. She rolled up her sleeves.

"She's getting pretty weak," Johnny said. His ruddy, freckled face showed his concern. He brushed a lock of his curly red hair back from his forehead. "Hilda's a nice little goat. I'd hate to lose her."

Rebecca heard a sob from the corner. Turning around, she saw the girl for the first time.

"Hilda's going to die—isn't she, Doctor?" the child asked, tears rolling down her cheeks. "I knew something awful was going to happen. And it is."

Rebecca walked over to the girl and patted her shiny black hair. "My name is Rebecca," she told her. "What's yours?"

"Katie," she said with a sniffle.

"Well, Katie, I don't think you need to worry too much about Hilda," Rebecca said. "I run into this sort of problem all the time. It usually works out just fine."

"Really?" The girl choked back her sobs. "You do it all the time?"

"Ten times yesterday," Rebecca replied with a smile.

The child laughed in spite of her tears. "I don't think it happens *that* often," she said.

"I think you're right. But she's going to be fine. You'll see."

Having comforted the child, Rebecca returned to Johnny and Hilda. She rubbed the cream all over her hands and arms, up to her elbows. Then she pulled on a pair of long rubber gloves.

"I'll check and see what's going on in there," she said. "We need to know what we're dealing with."

As Rebecca examined her patient, the animal lay still, too weak to resist.

"Well, we have twins," she said. "And the first one is a big fellow. He's the one who's holding up the works."

"What are you going to do?" Johnny asked.

"I'm going to turn him around a bit to get him into the proper position. Then I can ease him out."

Rebecca performed her task as gently as she could. Hilda seemed to sense that something had changed. She began to bear down again and push.

Chapter 3

A few minutes later, Rebecca delivered the first kid. As she had said, he was huge. But he didn't seem any the worse for his ordeal.

From the corner of her eye, Rebecca watched Katie leave her spot by the wall and inch toward them.

"Is it a boy or a girl?" the child asked. Her tears were gone, but her blue eyes were still big and round with wonder.

"It's a billy," Rebecca said. "A fine, strapping fellow. I certainly won't want to mess with him in another year or so."

Katie looked disappointed. "Oh. I was hoping for a girl."

Johnny laughed. "I promised her she could have one of the kids for a pet if it was a nanny."

"Well, there's one more left in there," Rebecca said. "And we'll know soon whether it's your nanny."

Katie lost her shyness. She scrambled to Rebecca's side and knelt on the straw. Reaching out her small hand, she stroked the goat's belly. "You're okay, Hilda," she said in a soft, soothing voice. "The nice doctor is going to take care of you."

"Yes," said a deep voice from behind them. "It looks like everything is under control."

Rebecca glanced over her shoulder and caught her breath. The man who stood in the doorway was the most handsome she had ever seen. With his shining black hair and blue eyes, it was clear that he was Katie's father. He almost filled the doorway with his broad shoulders. And the room seemed to vibrate with his presence.

But Rebecca didn't have time to think about a handsome man at the moment. As attractive as he was, she had work to do. The second kid was making its way into the world.

Rebecca felt a pang of concern when she saw the baby. It was much smaller than its brother. And it seemed limp and lifeless as she eased it out onto the straw.

Rebecca grabbed a handful of hay and began to rub the kid with quick, firm strokes. "Come on, little one," she whispered. "Let's get you going. Breathe for me—come on."

She noticed that it was a female and her heart sank. Katie would be crushed if it didn't live.

Just when Rebecca was about to give it CPR, the tiny animal gave a shudder. It gasped for air and kicked its hind legs.

"There she goes," Johnny said, his face breaking into a wide grin. "You did it, Doc!" He grabbed Katie and gave her a bear hug.

"And it's a girl!" Katie said. "It's a little nanny—for *me!*"

"That's right, Katie," Johnny said. "A bonny nanny for a bonny lass."

Hilda raised her head to look down at her twins. She wore a tired and interested look on her face. Her long

Nubian ears flopped as she reached out and licked her offspring.

Both kids snuggled close to their mother, seeking her warm milk.

Rebecca sat down in the straw and enjoyed the scene. *This* was why she had become a vet. Moments like this. Hilda was relieved of her burden. The kids were safe and cozy. Katie and Johnny were thrilled with the new arrivals. And Katie's father . . .

Rebecca turned to see if he was enjoying this warm scene as much as they were. But to her surprise, he wore a frown on his handsome face.

He took a couple of steps toward them, then stopped. "That goat is a runt," he said, looking down at the newborn nanny. "I don't think it will make a good pet for a child."

"She is so a good pet. I want her!" Katie said. She stared up at her father, her blue eyes pleading. "And she's *not* a runt—whatever that is."

Rebecca had to fight to control her temper. What was wrong with this man? Didn't he have a heart? How could he ruin such a beautiful, happy moment?

"A runt is unhealthy," he told his daughter. "It will be hard to care for. And you don't even know if she'll live."

Rebecca couldn't stay quiet any longer. "Excuse me, Mr.—"

"Stafford," he said. "Michael Stafford."

"Mr. Stafford. I understand your concern about having a healthy pet for your child. But even though this one is a bit small, there's no reason to think it won't live."

"Oh, really?" His blue eyes were cold as he glared down at her. He seemed to resent her giving her opinion without being asked. "And can you guarantee that, Doctor?"

Rebecca couldn't understand the bitter tone of his voice. Why was he reacting this way? "Of course I can't promise the animal will stay healthy, Mr. Stafford," she said. "Life doesn't offer guarantees like that."

"It certainly doesn't," he replied.

Rebecca thought she heard anger in his voice. What had happened to this man to make him so cold?

Looking down at Katie, Rebecca could see the pain in her blue eyes. It seemed to run in the family.

"Mr. Stafford," she said, trying to sound patient. "I truly believe this goat is healthy, in spite of her small size. If you will allow Katie to have her as a pet, I promise to help all I can. I'll teach your daughter how to take care of a goat. And if anything goes wrong, all you have to do is call me. I'll be here right away."

"Please, Daddy?" Katie pleaded. She jumped up from the straw and ran to her father. Taking his hand, she said, "Dr. Barclay thinks it's okay. Let me have her. Please, please, please."

Michael Stafford looked down at his daughter, who was tugging at his hand. Rebecca couldn't believe he could resist those big blue eyes.

He couldn't. He pulled his hand away and turned toward the door. "Well," he said as he walked away, "if Dr. Barclay thinks it's okay, it must be okay. I'm sure she knows more about these things than I do. I only hope she's right this time."

Rebecca wished he hadn't sounded so sarcastic. But he had given in, and that was what counted.

Rising, Rebecca began to gather her things into her bag. Her work here was finished. At least for the moment.

When she was ready to walk out the door, she paused. She turned to take one more look at Hilda, the baby goats, Katie, and Johnny. Katie had her arms around the baby nanny's neck and was saying sweet things in her ear.

Yes, Rebecca thought, *I knew there were reasons why I became a vet. This is one of them.*

Chapter 4

For the next week, Rebecca couldn't stop thinking about Katie, Michael Stafford, and the baby goat. Finally, she gave in to her worries and dropped by Casa Colina.

The warm summer sun made her feel lazy as she got out of her pickup and walked up to the house. It was the perfect summer morning to just sit in the sun and sip iced tea.

She sighed to herself. No such luck. The busy life of a vet didn't offer her much time to relax.

She found Katie and the kid romping in the backyard. Playing a game of tag, they seemed to be enjoying each other's company.

"Hi, Dr. Barclay!" Katie shouted as she ran toward Rebecca.

"Hello, Katie." Rebecca reached down to pet the goat. It lowered its tiny head and butted against her palm. "I see you've been teaching her bad habits," Rebecca teased.

"I didn't have to teach her that," Katie said with a giggle. "She seemed to know it all by herself."

"Yes, goats are little rascals. You have to teach them to behave. How is she doing?"

"Oh, fine," Katie said. "I named her Rosebud. But I call her Rosie."

"Rosie . . . hmm . . . ," Rebecca said thoughtfully. She studied the little goat, its silky white coat, long floppy ears, blue eyes, and pink nose. "Rosebud. Yes, I like that name. It's perfect for her."

Katie beamed at the praise. "I'm out of school now for the summer," she said. "We play all the time. She's my best friend."

Rebecca looked around for signs of another human being. In the distance, Johnny was digging in the garden. And his wife, Linda, stood in the kitchen window. Michael Stafford must have allowed her to stay on as housekeeper.

But Katie's father was nowhere in sight. And Rebecca was sorry to see that Katie had no other children to play with.

"So, it's just you and Rosie?" she asked the girl. "No people friends to play with?"

The girl looked sad for a moment, then shook her head. Her black curls bounced and shone in the sunlight.

"Nope. Just me and Rosie. I don't have any other friends."

"Don't you ever invite the kids from school to come over?" Rebecca asked. She thought of all the wonderful times she had shared with the Flores girls here at the casa.

"I used to have friends over to play," Katie said. She wouldn't look up at Rebecca as she bent to scratch Rosie's ear. "But that was before. You know— when my mommy was alive."

Pain shot through Rebecca. The pain of loss was always so close to her heart.

"I'm sorry, Katie," she said. She stroked the girl's shining hair. "It's hard to lose someone you love. I know."

Katie looked up at her with curious eyes. "Really? Did someone *you* love die, too?"

"Yes. My husband," Rebecca said sadly. "We had only been married two years."

"Was he sick for a long time?" Katie asked.

So, Rebecca thought, *that's how her mother died. A long illness.*

"No," she said. "He was in a car accident."

"Oh." Katie nodded gravely in understanding. "That must have been awful. You didn't even get to say goodbye."

"No, I didn't," Rebecca agreed. "I think that was the worst part."

Katie looked away, as though remembering. "My daddy told me to tell my mommy goodbye," she said. "But I cried, and I wouldn't do it. I was just a dumb seven-year-old. Now I'm eight, and I'm a lot more mature."

"Yes, I can see that," Rebecca said with a smile. "But you shouldn't blame yourself. Everyone finds it hard to tell someone they love goodbye. I don't think you were a dumb seven-year-old.

I just think you were really scared. That's all."

Katie's eyes brimmed with tears, but she smiled up at Rebecca. "That's nice," she said. "Maybe that's all it was."

"I'm sure of it."

"Want to see something really neat?" Katie asked, suddenly light-hearted.

"Sure, what is it?" Rebecca said, happy to change the subject.

"Just wait until you see this. It's really funny."

The girl ran over to a nearby plum tree and picked a piece of the fruit. Rebecca had a feeling she knew what was going to happen. But she didn't say so.

"Watch this!" Katie said as she held the plum out to Rosebud.

Rebecca had seen goats eat peaches and plums before. She knew what was coming.

The goat rolled the fruit around in its mouth for a couple of seconds. Then she spit the seed out—perfectly clean. As the pit sailed through the air, Katie cackled with glee.

"Did you see that?" she said. "She gets *all* the plum off the seed and spits it really far!"

"Most impressive," Rebecca agreed. "A lot of boys I know would like to be able to spit that far."

Katie giggled again, and Rebecca thought what a beautiful child she was. Why didn't her father take more of an interest in her?

"So, has your dad seen Rosie do this?" Rebecca asked.

Katie's smile disappeared. "No. He's almost never around. He works a lot at his car place in Los Angeles."

"Car place?"

"Yeah. He sells really expensive cars that he gets from Europe." Katie looked away, as though remembering again. "He used to be home a lot. He used to play with me and Mommy and make us pancakes in the morning. But now he just works all the time."

Rebecca recalled the months after her husband's accident. She had spent long hours trying to escape into her job. It hadn't worked. Sooner or later, she had to stop working and go to bed. Alone. And then she couldn't avoid the memories.

"I miss my mom," Katie said. "But I miss my dad, too. I wish he was around more."

Rebecca felt a rush of anger toward the man who could neglect this child. When her husband, Tim, had died, she had been so lonely. If only she had been left with a beautiful reminder of him—like Katie. She certainly wouldn't have deserted the child, no matter how much pain she had suffered.

"Have you told your father how you feel?" Rebecca asked.

"No." Katie shrugged her small shoulders. "I don't want to make him feel bad. He's sad enough already."

"Maybe you should tell him," Rebecca said gently. "Maybe he doesn't know that you're feeling sad, too. It always helps if you have someone to feel sad with."

Katie considered her words for a moment. Then she shook her head. "No. I'll just talk to Rosebud. She doesn't have as much to worry about as my dad does."

Rebecca glanced at her watch. She had another stop to make. "I have to go now, Katie. But I'll come by again soon to check on you two."

Katie seemed disappointed, but she nodded. "Okay. Thanks for coming over." She blushed and stared down at her purple and pink sneakers. "I mean . . . Rosie likes you and she was glad to see you."

"I like her, too," Rebecca said with a smile. "Very much."

Rebecca said her goodbyes and walked around to the front of the house. As she was about to step into her pickup, a late model Jaguar pulled into the drive.

Michael Stafford climbed out, looking as striking as he had the other night. He wore a charcoal suit and a white silk shirt. His dark hair was combed back. But one lock had escaped and hung boyishly over his forehead.

The look in his blue eyes was anything but boyish. He gave her a curt nod of his head, but no smile of greeting.

"Good morning, Mr. Stafford," Rebecca said. She sounded much more friendly than she felt.

"What's wrong?" he asked. "Has something happened to the goat?"

"No, not at all," she assured him. "I was just dropping by to say hello to Katie."

He looked relieved, but still angry. "I haven't changed my mind, Dr. Barclay. I believe it was a mistake to let her keep that mangy goat," he said. "My daughter is obsessed with the thing. If it were to get sick or . . ."

"Yes?" she asked, her temper rising.

"Or die, she would be crushed. And I can tell you now, Doctor, I'll blame you if it happens."

That did it. Rebecca could no longer control her tongue. She knew she was about to say things she would regret later.

"Mr. Stafford," she said, gritting her teeth, "your daughter needs a living being to love. Maybe she wouldn't be so obsessed with a goat if her father spent a little time with her."

She turned and stomped back to her truck. "And by the way," she added,

"Rosie isn't mangy. *None* of *my* patients have mange, thank you!" She climbed in and slammed the door behind her.

She pulled away, tires squealing. In her rearview mirror she could see him standing in a cloud of dust. His mouth was hanging open.

"So there, Michael Stafford," she said, quite pleased with herself. "Just put *that* in your pipe and smoke it!"

Chapter 5

Autumn arrived in its usual California fashion. Except for the dry Santa Ana winds and the calendar on her wall, Rebecca couldn't even tell it was fall.

This was the only time of year when she wished she lived in New England. She longed for the brightly colored trees and the scent of burning leaves in the crisp air.

But one San Carlos fall tradition she enjoyed was the county fair. As the local vet, she was always asked to judge the dog, cat, and rabbit shows. Handing out the blue ribbons was a high point of her year.

She arrived at the fair early on Saturday morning. She looked around her and soaked in the sights and sounds. Children were walking their animals down the gangway. Winners displayed their prize flowers, cakes and pies, and needlework of all kinds. Some of the men displayed their leather crafts and woodworking.

Rebecca said hello to almost everyone she met. San Carlos was small enough that she knew most of its citizens.

As Rebecca neared the livestock area, she saw Katie. The girl was leading Rosebud by a small leather bridle. Rosie was decked out with pink ribbons, bells, and bows on her tail and around her neck. The goat was behaving quite well. She seemed proud of herself as she pranced along behind her mistress.

Most surprising of all, Rebecca saw Michael Stafford walking beside his daughter and her pet. He looked almost as proud as they did. He wore a broad, carefree smile. And he seemed more relaxed than Rebecca had ever seen him.

"Hi, Dr. Barclay!" Katie shouted across the way. "Look, Daddy. It's Dr. Barclay!"

"So it is," Michael said. He gave Rebecca a dazzling smile that nearly stopped her heart. "How are you today, Doctor?"

"Ah . . . fine, thank you," Rebecca replied, suddenly feeling shy and awkward.

"Look what we won!" Katie said as she held up a red ribbon. "Rosie won second place!"

"A red ribbon! Good for you, Katie." Rebecca scratched the top of the nanny's head. "You deserve it. She looks beautiful today!"

"Daddy helped." Katie beamed up at her father. "She wouldn't hold still when I was giving her a bath. So he helped me chase her around."

Rebecca's eyes met Michael's.

For just a moment he seemed embarrassed. Then he shrugged. "A red ribbon isn't too bad," he said, "for a mangy runt. Is it, Doc?"

"Not bad at all," Rebecca replied.

Michael looked down at Katie and patted her shoulder. "Why don't you and Rosebud go ahead," he said. "I want to talk to Dr. Barclay for a minute. I'll be right there."

Katie looked from her father to Rebecca and back. A grin played across her face. "Sure, Dad. No problem," she said.

As soon as Katie and the goat were gone, Michael seemed even more nervous than before.

"I . . . ah . . . ," he began.

"Yes, Mr. Stafford?"

"I wanted to thank you for what you said the other day. I don't mind telling you, I was furious with you then. But I thought about it, and I decided you were right. I have been neglecting Katie."

He took a deep breath. Rebecca could see the pain in his eyes. She remembered Tim and how she had felt for the first year after he died.

"I lost my husband, too," she said. "I felt some of what you're going through. I know it's a difficult time."

"Yes, it is. But that doesn't excuse the way I acted about the little goat. I don't know why I said what I did and . . ."

His voice trailed off, and Rebecca could see the guilt in his eyes.

"I was afraid for Katie," he said. "I thought the goat might be sick. I didn't want her to lose something else she loved. I guess I over-reacted. But she's lost so much already."

"I understand." Rebecca wondered if she should say what was on her mind. She would risk making him angry again. But she felt she should be honest with him.

"Mr. Stafford," she said. "I don't claim to know everything you're feeling. But if you over-reacted, I think it's because you love your daughter so much."

"Yes, I do," he said. "And her mother's death was very hard for her."

Rebecca nodded. "I know you're afraid of her suffering another loss. And you don't want her to love something that could die. But Katie can't close her heart. She has too much love to give. And so do you," she added quietly.

He said nothing, but stared down at the sawdust on the ground.

"To love a living being is to risk getting hurt," she continued. "Because we all die, sooner or later. But there is one thing that's worse than losing someone you love. That's not having loved anyone at all."

She couldn't tell how her words had affected him. He just kept staring at the ground.

"I know you're afraid to feel your love for Katie," she said. If she was going to upset him, she might as well go all the way. "But there are more ways to lose someone than through death. We can lose the people we love, even though we see them every day."

He cleared his throat and nodded curtly. "Yes. Of course you're right, Dr. Barclay. But I have to get going. Katie needs help loading Rosebud into the trailer."

Before she could reply, he was gone.

"Way to go, Rebecca," she muttered. "You sure have a great way with people. Maybe you'd better stick to fuzzy-faced critters that can't talk."

Chapter 6

Rebecca lay in bed, dreaming that she could hear a ship's horn across a foggy sea. One, two, three blasts. Then she realized it wasn't a ship at all. It was the telephone.

Another call in the middle of the night.

"This is getting old," she mumbled as she reached for the phone. "Yes?" she asked, trying to shake herself awake.

"Rebecca, this is Michael Stafford."

She sat up in bed, instantly alert. Even in her half-asleep state she realized that he had called her by her first name. And she had heard the worried tone of his voice. Something was very wrong.

"Yes, Michael," she said. "What is it?"

"Rosebud is very sick. I don't know what's wrong with her. Johnny is gone for the weekend. And Katie . . . well . . . Katie is terribly upset."

"I'll be right there."

Rebecca jumped out of bed and threw on her clothes. Fear rose in her chest, but she tried to push it down.

"Not Rosie," she whispered. "Please, not that one. Katie really needs her."

She would do everything she could to help. She prayed it would be enough.

Chapter 7

Rosebud was even worse than she had expected. Rebecca's heart sank as she knelt in the straw and examined the little goat. Her stomach was badly swollen. She was crying pitifully and was unable to move.

"What's wrong with her, Doctor?" Katie said as tears ran down her cheeks. "Is she going to die?"

Rebecca wanted to tell her everything was going to be fine, as she had before. But she wouldn't lie to the child. This time she wasn't sure at all. She didn't even know what was wrong.

She asked the normal questions. Katie and Michael gave the answers. But none of those replies gave her the information she needed.

Quickly Rebecca ran the symptoms through her head. She tried to match them with an illness or injury that she had studied.

"Wait a minute," she said at last. "Do you have an avocado tree on the property?"

Katie and Michael looked at each other.

"Yes," Michael said. "We have two— far back against the fence."

"Could Rosebud have eaten some of the leaves today?" Rebecca asked Katie.

"Well . . . Dad and I went out for ice cream," Katie said, reaching for her father's hand. "I left her in the backyard while we were gone. I guess she could have eaten some then."

"I need to know for sure," Rebecca said.

Michael jumped to his feet. "I'll check," he said. He rushed out of the barn toward the backyard.

A moment later he returned. He held a half-eaten avocado and some munched leaves in his hand. "I'm afraid she's been at it," he said. "Is that bad?"

Rebecca couldn't bring herself to tell them that she had lost several horses this way. Avocado leaves were deadly to animals. Why hadn't she warned Katie before?

"Rosie can't digest the leaves," she told them. "That's the problem. They say goats can eat anything. And that's true—almost. Even a goat's stomach can't handle avocado leaves."

"What can we do?" Michael asked.

"We have to help her get rid of them," Rebecca said. "Even if it takes all night."

"How do we do that?" Katie asked.

Rebecca smiled down at the girl. "You may think this is silly," she said. "But the old-fashioned way is the best. Do you guys have a turkey baster?"

"A *turkey baster?*" Michael asked.

"Yes, that's what we need."

He thought for a moment. "I think so. Somewhere."

"Well, get it," Rebecca said, rolling up her sleeves. "We have work to do."

Chapter 8

Michael watched Rebecca fill the baster
with mineral oil and milk of magnesia.
Gently he held the nanny's mouth open
as Rebecca squeezed the mixture in.
Rosie swallowed weakly, then began to
cry again.

They had been giving her the
medicine for the past four hours. But so
far, there had been no results.

"Do you really think this is going to help?" Michael asked.

"I don't know yet," Rebecca said, putting the baster aside. "If we can just get enough into her, it may all work out . . . in the end." She pointed to Rosie's tail.

"A bad pun, Dr. Barclay," Michael said with a tired smile.

"Hey, at four o'clock in the morning that's as good as it gets."

Rebecca looked over at Katie, who was sleeping in the corner. She was curled into a ball in the straw. Michael's leather jacket was draped over her small shoulders.

"She finally gave it up, huh?" Rebecca said.

"Yes, and I'm glad," Michael replied. "There was no reason for her to be up all night worrying."

He gazed at the child for a long time. Then he turned back to Rebecca. "You were right, you know . . . at the fair.

I really am afraid I'm going to lose her, too. I wake up in the middle of the night sweating, worrying about it."

Rebecca nodded. "I know. It's perfectly normal. You'll feel that way for a while. But as time passes, it does get easier."

"Really?" He looked at her with a light of hope in his blue eyes.

"Yes, I promise. The first two years are the worst. Then it gets easier."

Michael ran his hand over the kid's swollen belly. Rebecca noticed that his fingers were shaking slightly. Her heart went out to him. She wondered how she could have thought he was cold and uncaring.

"When I think of my wife," he said, "I only remember her death . . . the last time I saw her. I don't want to think of her that way."

"Time will help you with that," Rebecca said. She laid a comforting hand on his shoulder. "Someday you'll remember her life more than her death."

At her touch, Michael turned to her as though seeing her for the first time. "You're really someone special, Dr. Barclay," he said. "You have the gift of healing."

Rebecca gave him a puzzled look.

"It seems," he said, "that you help to mend people's broken hearts as well as animals."

"I only wish that were true," she said. "But from what I've seen, the only true healers are time and hope."

Rosie gave a loud bleat and tried to stand.

"Hey, hey," Rebecca said. "This looks hopeful."

Michael rose from his seat on the straw. "Here," he said, "let me help her stand up."

Carefully, he lifted the nanny and supported her. When he released her,

her legs were wobbly, but she was standing. And that was what mattered for now.

"Now we wait again," Rebecca said. "She seems to be ready to do something."

A few minutes later, the medicine finally worked. The little animal rid herself of most of her burden. She had stopped crying. Her tiny tail had even begun to wag a bit.

"What a good girl!" Rebecca cried. She dropped to her knees and hugged the goat around the neck. "Your mistress will be so proud of you when she wakes up."

"Should I tell her?" Michael said, nodding toward Katie.

"I wouldn't," Rebecca said. "In another hour or two, Rosie will be feeling even better and ready to play. Why don't you let Katie sleep until then."

Michael walked over to his daughter. He tucked the jacket more snugly around her shoulders and neck. Then he stroked her black, shining curls.

"You were right about something else," he said. "Even if I lose her someday, I wouldn't have missed having Katie in my life. She's given me so much joy."

"I can imagine," Rebecca said.

"But I was so afraid to love her the way I loved her mother," he said. "But just look at her. How could I help it?"

Rebecca smiled. "I know what you mean. She's a wonderful child. I've grown very fond of her in only a short time."

"Well, that feeling seems to be mutual," he said. "All the way around."

His eyes met hers. She felt more tenderness than she had felt for a long time. But her rush of happiness was quickly followed by a pang of fear.

It never went away completely . . . the fear of loving . . . of losing.

But something in his eyes gave her the courage to push the fear away. At least for the moment. She held out her hand to him.

"I'm glad," she said. "I've enjoyed knowing you, your daughter—and even Rosebud." Rebecca laughed. "Although I wish she would be more careful what she eats."

He returned her smile. "Speaking of eating—are you hungry?"

"Starved."

"Then I should invite you to join us for a family tradition," he said.

"And what's that?"

Before he could answer, Katie sprang up from her bed in the straw. She looked sleepy and tired, but thrilled.

"Rosebud!" she shouted. "You're standing! You're not crying anymore!"

She threw her father's jacket aside and ran to her pet. The goat's tail began to wag as she nuzzled her mistress.

"You made her well!" the child cried as she hugged the animal. "Dr. Barclay, you fixed her! Thank you! Thank you *so* much!"

"You're welcome, Katie," Rebecca replied. "But I couldn't have done it alone. I had a lot of help." She nodded toward Michael.

Katie glowed with pride as she looked at her father. It was clear he was her hero at that moment. She walked over to him and wrapped her arms around his waist. "Thanks, Daddy," she said.

"You're welcome, kiddo." He returned her hug, then tugged on one of her curls. "I was just about to ask Dr. Barclay if she wants to have pancakes with us this morning."

"Really?" Katie's smile grew even wider. "Your special pancakes?"

"With pineapple and pecans and maple syrup," he said, looking at Rebecca.

"Sounds great!" she agreed. "I accept."

Katie hurried over to Rebecca and motioned for her to lean down. Placing her lips against her ear, the girl whispered, "He doesn't make his special pancakes for just anybody. I think he likes you."

"Hmm . . . that's nice," was all Rebecca could say. She felt the blood rushing to her cheeks and turning them bright red.

"What are you two whispering about?" Michael asked.

"Nothing." Katie giggled and gave Rosebud a kiss on her pink nose. "I'll go put the syrup in the microwave," she said. "That's my job when we make pancakes."

She took off, running and skipping toward the house.

Rebecca felt awkward being alone with Michael. Katie had said that he liked her. And the look on his face told her the same thing. How embarrassing, how strange . . . how nice.

Maybe the strangest thing of all was that she was pretty sure she liked him, too.

"Thanks for making me look good with the kid," he said.

"No problem," she replied. "But I do charge more for that. It'll be on my bill."

"So, I'll owe you, huh, Doc?" He lifted one eyebrow.

"Big time."

He took her hand and led her out of the stable. She didn't resist. Why should she, when it felt so natural, so right?

"I might have to pay you off in pancakes," he said, squeezing her hand.

"Pineapple pancakes . . ." She thought for a moment. "Okay. I'll consider it a down payment."

JANET DAILEY'S

LOVE SCENES

Janet Dailey's Love Scenes
is a collection of short, easy-to-read
stories of love and romance by Janet
Dailey and other authors.

For a free catalog of this series and
other Signal Hill books and tapes,
please write:

Signal Hill Publications
Box 131
Syracuse, NY 13210-0131

SIGNAL HILL